The Last Hazelnut

written by Susanna Isern

illustrated by Mariana Ruiz Johnson

translated by María A. Pérez

Barefoot Books
step inside a story

Tim and Teo meet one day in the forest.

"Hi, Teo! I was looking for you. I've just picked some hazelnuts. Shall we share them?"

"What a great idea, Tim! I love hazelnuts!"

Tim and Teo climb to
the top of the mountain.

When they get there,
they sit down together.

They love to spend time together at the top of the mountain.

"Yummy!"

"Yes, they're delicious!"

"Teo, there is nothing better than eating hazelnuts on a mountaintop."

"I think so too, Tim."

"You're so selfish!"

"You're such a bad friend!"

Tim is furious. When he gets home, he throws away everything that reminds him of Teo.

Teo is also very angry. He gets rid of everything connected to Tim.

That night, Tim has trouble sleeping.

"How could Teo have eaten the last hazelnut?"

Teo can't sleep either.

"I can't believe Tim would eat the
last hazelnut without telling me."

In the morning,
Tim goes for a walk.

Teo decides
to take a stroll.

Tim finds a ball in the ground.

"If Teo were here, he'd dig it up in a flash and then we could play."

Teo comes across a pair of binoculars hanging from a tree branch.

"If Tim were here, he'd get them in a single leap and then
we could see what's on the other side of the woods."

Tim climbs up a hazel tree.

"All of this over one hazelnut?"

Teo sits by the lake.

"This isn't worth fighting over."

Tim climbs down the hazel tree and runs to look for Teo.

Teo leaves the lake and runs to look for Tim.

"I'm sorry about what happened, Teo."

"Me too, Tim. Let's just forget about it."

"I agree. I've just picked some more hazelnuts.
Shall we share them?"

"I'd love to."

Tim and Teo climb to
the top of the mountain.

When they get there,
they sit down together.

From the top, they can see other mountains and forests.

"Very tasty!"

"Yes, they're great!"

"Teo, I still think there is nothing better than eating hazelnuts on a mountaintop."

"I think so too, Tim."

"Come on, Teo. The last hazelnut is for you."

"No, you eat it, Tim."

"I've got an idea, Teo! Let's split the hazelnut in half."

"What a great idea, Tim!"

"You know what, Teo? It feels good to share."

"I totally agree, Tim. Now shall
we roll down the mountain together?"

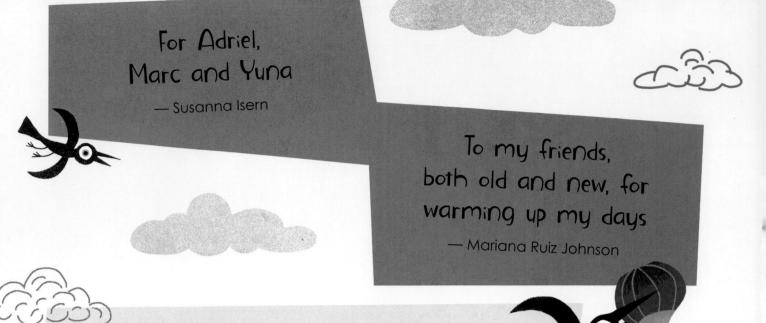

For Adriel,
Marc and Yuna
— Susanna Isern

To my friends,
both old and new, for
warming up my days
— Mariana Ruiz Johnson

Barefoot Books
2067 Massachusetts Ave
Cambridge, MA 02140

Barefoot Books
29/30 Fitzroy Square
London, W1T 6LQ

First published in the United States of America by Barefoot Books, Inc
and in Great Britain by Barefoot Books, Ltd in 2020

Graphic design by Elizabeth Kaleko, Barefoot Books
English edition edited by Kate DePalma
Translated by María A. Pérez
Reproduction by Bright Arts, Hong Kong
Printed in China on 100% acid-free paper
This book was typeset in Century Gothic, Fini and Pinch
The illustrations were prepared in mixed media
combined with digital techniques

Hardback ISBN 978-1-64686-055-5
Paperback ISBN 978-1-64686-056-2
E-book ISBN 978-1-64686-079-1

British Cataloguing-in-Publication Data:
a catalogue record for this book is available from the British Library

Library of Congress Cataloging-in-Publication Data
is available under LCCN 2020003248

1 3 5 7 9 8 6 4 2

Barefoot Books
Step inside a Story

At Barefoot Books, we celebrate art and story that opens the hearts
and minds of children from all walks of life, focusing on themes that
encourage independence of spirit, enthusiasm for learning and respect
for the world's diversity. The welfare of our children is dependent on
the welfare of the planet, so we source paper from sustainably managed
forests and constantly strive to reduce our environmental impact.
Playful, beautiful and created to last a lifetime, our products combine
the best of the present with the best of the past to educate our
children as the caretakers of tomorrow.

www.barefootbooks.com

Susanna Isern

is a writer, psychologist and mother of three. She is the author of more than 60 children's books, which are available all around the world and have been translated into over a dozen languages. Susanna lives in Santander, Spain.

Mariana Ruiz Johnson

is an award-winning children's book illustrator and author. She lives on the outskirts of Buenos Aires, Argentina with her husband and two children. Mariana has also illustrated *Head, Shoulders, Knees and Toes* for Barefoot Books.